THIS LITTLE PIGGY

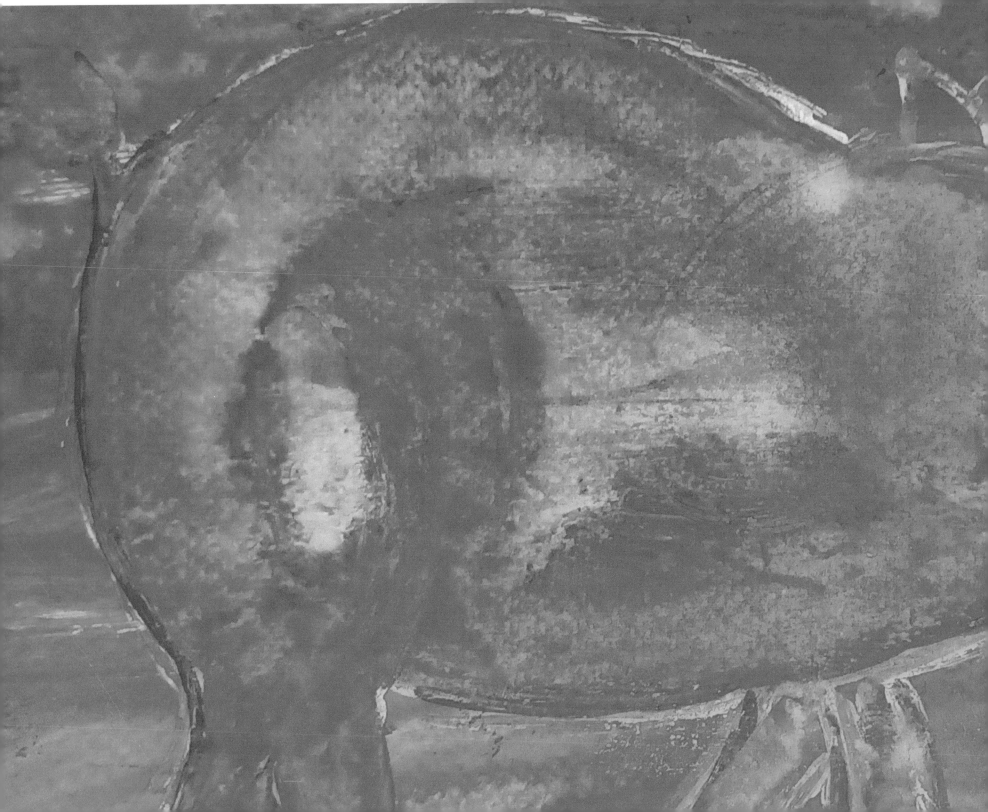

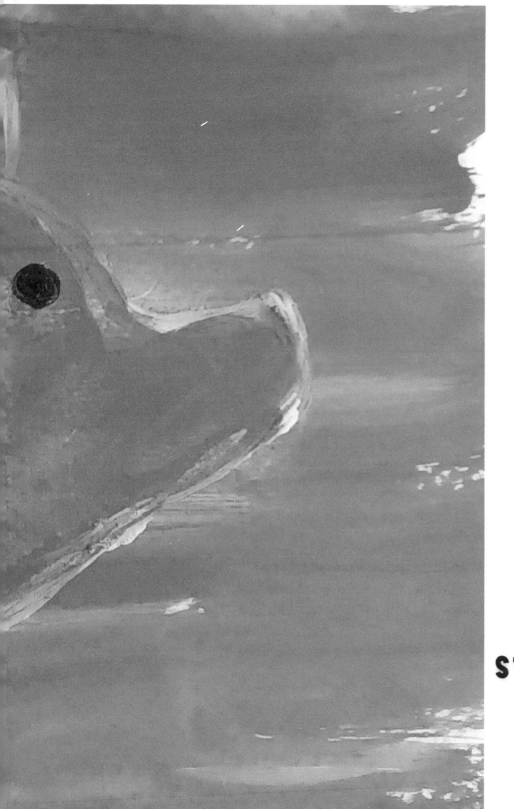

THIS LITTLE PIGGY

story and illustrations by

CHRISTINA KING

This little piggy was brave.

She rode her bike fast, climbed trees, and swam in the deep end of the pool.

This little piggy was beautiful.

She had the best hair and always wore the most fashionable outfits.

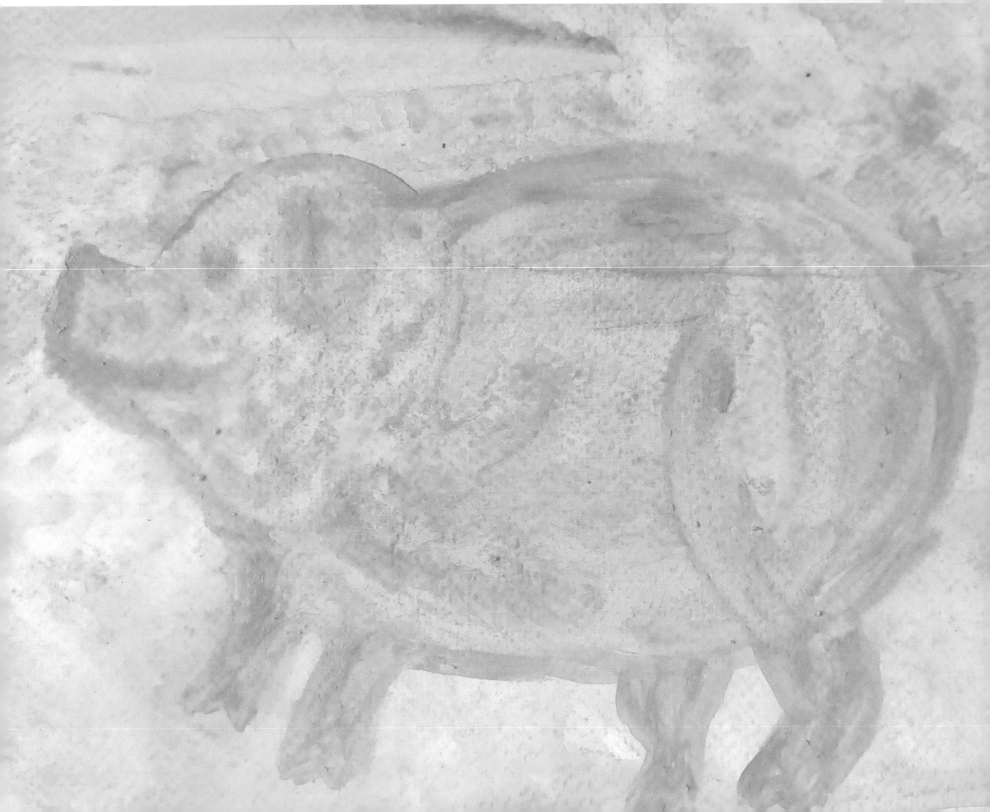

This little piggy was smart.

She read lots of books, studied hard, and got all As on her report card.

This little piggy was . . . not brave.

She was . . . not beautiful.

She was . . . not smart.

This little piggy was cute.

He was super little and sweet,

He was the baby piggy.

The fourth little piggy was . . . not cute.

"What kind of piggy am I?" said the fourth little piggy.

She thought and thought and thought about what kind of piggy she was for a long time.

Surely, there must be something special about her.

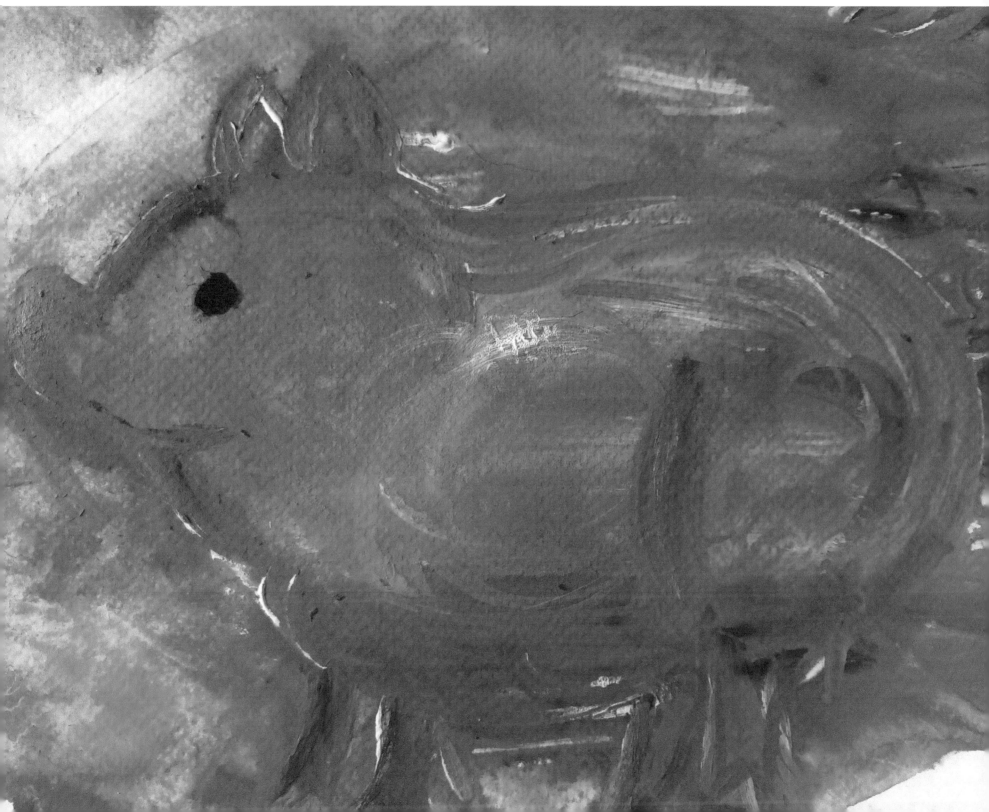

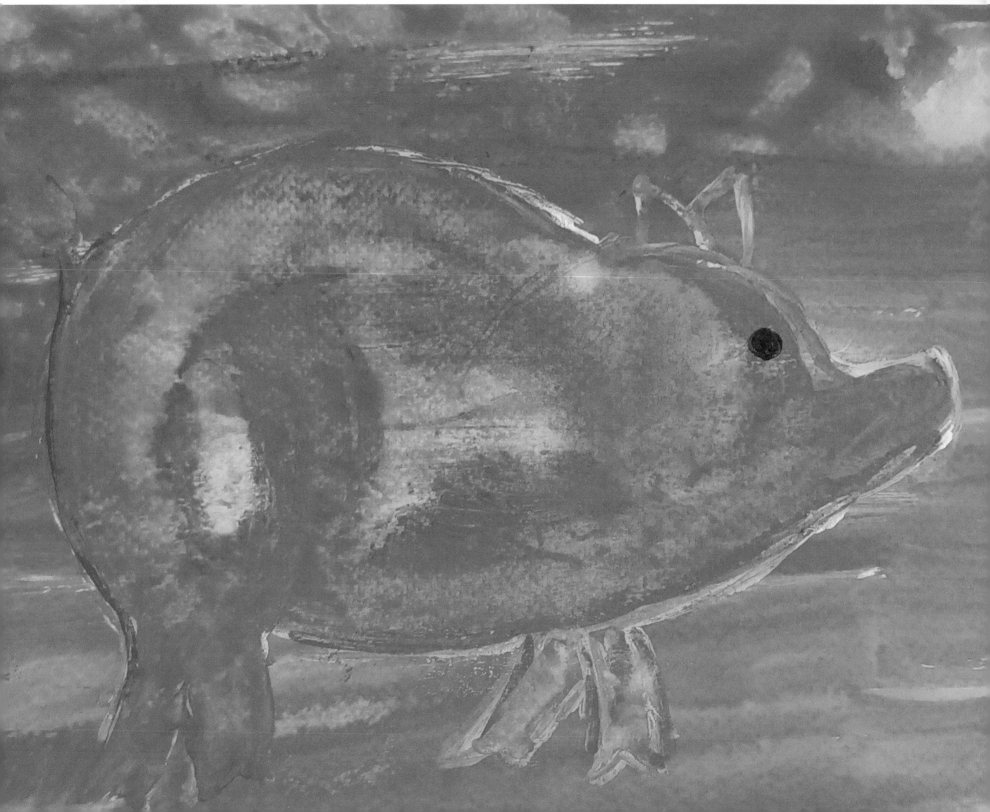

She decided she would be
the kindest piggy!

So, the little piggy decided to be kind whenever she could because being kind is something you can choose to be.

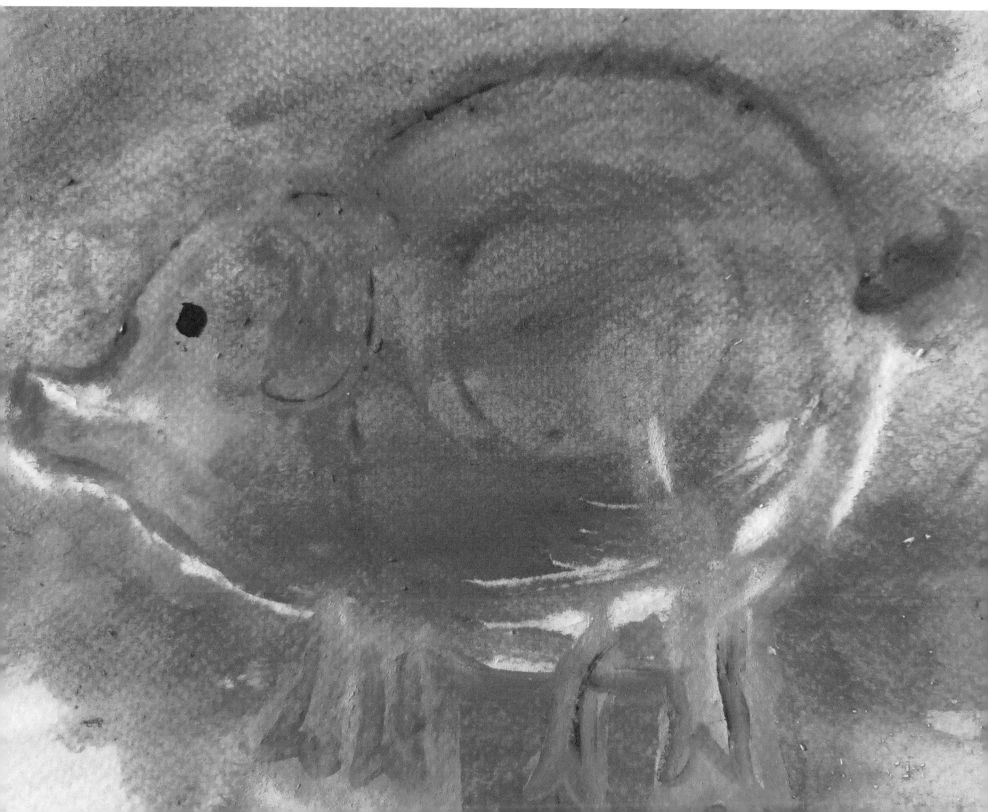

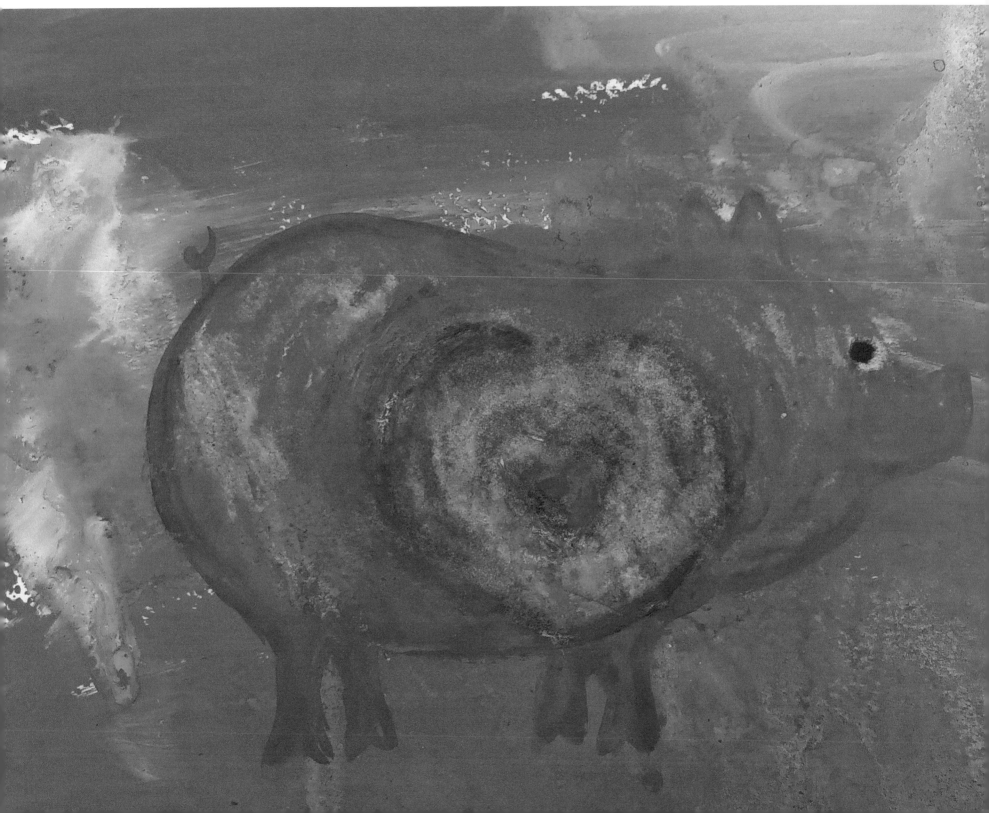

Being kind to others made the little piggy happy.

She felt a glow inside her heart that made her proud to be who she was.

She discovered she didn't have to be the most brave, beautiful, smartest, or cutest.

She was special in her own way.

The fourth little piggy was the happiest piggy because she was the kindest piggy.

And being yourself is the bravest, smartest, and most beautiful of all!

Be You. Be Kind.

Printed in the USA
CPSIA information can be obtained
at www.ICGtesting.com
LVHW060109151023

761014LV00048B/474